Digger!

A Catalogue record for this book is available from the British Library.

ISBN 13: 978-0-9559711-8-1

Reproduction by Digital Sunrise UK

Printed in Belgium by Proost

Caboodle Books Ltd
Riversdale, 8 Rivock Avenue, Steeton, BD20 6SA

Tel: 01535 656015

Digger!

Written and Illustrated by Liz Million

Caboodle Books

Digger was busy tidying the school desks with the help of his sister and brothers . It was home time at last.
Mrs Spot reminded the the young dinosaurs about their homework task that had to be done at the weekend.
"I would like everyone to write about what they want to be when they grow up" she said.

Oooh, OOOh! I already know what I'm going to be, Miss!

"Why don't you write and tell me all about it, Jake" said Mrs Spot.

On the way home the excited little dinosaurs were all telling their Mummy about what they were going to be when they grew up.

I am going to be a top gymnast

Digger

I am going to be a swimming teacher, Mummy!

Ethan

Jake

Digger quietly plodded along. He was worried about his homework task.

"You're quiet today Digger. Is something the matter?" asked his Mummy gently. I don't know **what** I want to be when I grow up, Mummy" he mumbled "and I feel sad because everyone else seems to know what they want to be."

"Don't worry. I am sure we can think of something over the weekend'

Digger found his Daddy happily cooking meatballs in the kitchen. "What did you want to be when you were little, Daddy?" asked Digger. His Daddy thought for a while and smiled. "I **always** wanted to be a fire fighter who could rescue kittens from tall trees and put out big fires" smiled his Daddy gazing into the distance. "Now the **only** fires I get to put out are the ones in my cafe when I burn the food" he laughed.

That night Digger slept badly. "I am not **really** very good at **anything**" he thought glumly.

Every Saturday Daddy walked the little dinosaurs to their various clubs. Digger didn't have a special club to go to so he stayed at home and waited for his Gran to arrive.

She visited the family home every Saturday without fail. It was
Digger's job to help her untangle her many balls of wool.
Gran was a brilliant knitter.

He raced upstairs to his bedroom and dug out exactly what he needed.

"I can practice my new sport every day in secret and then I will invent a cool name for it. It will involve juggling balls whilst bouncing on a space hopper so I had better put on protective clothing" chuckled Digger.

A very happy Digger bounced down the stairs and through the lounge. Mummy and Gran looked up to see a flash of blue whizzing past them.

Poor Digger couldn't see through Jake's old swimmimg goggles. He was going too fast to stop and see that Gran's wool was stretched across the hallway!

He glided through the air like a terrified superhero and landed on the kitchen worktop. Daddy's big pot of spaghetti and meatballs flew through the air!

The little dinosaur picked himself up and pulled off his ridiculous outfit with a sigh.

"I was only trying to be good at something...anything" sniffled Digger grumpily.

"We're pleased that you weren't hurt but just <u>look</u> at this mess Digger! I'm going to clean up your poor Gran and I want this kitchen tidy by the time I get back" said Mummy handing him a scrubbing brush and a bucket of soapy water.

Digger mopped the kitchen floor and picked up every strand of spaghetti. He started to daydream as he wiped the gloopy tomato sauce from the walls. He imagined what it would be like to be a famous artist who could create bright colours and paint them onto big walls.
He was so busy daydreaming he didn't hear the door opening behind him.

His family were surprised to see the masterpiece on the wall and so was Digger!

"Oh goodness! That is beautiful" gasped Gran

"Digger you are an artist!" said Rosie smiling

"An artist..." whispered Digger thoughtfully. "Now I know what I am going to be when I grow up" said Digger with a big toothy grin.

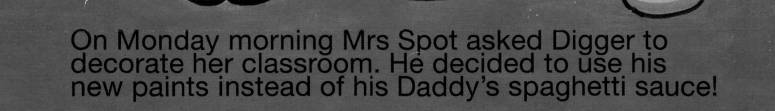

On Monday morning Mrs Spot asked Digger to decorate her classroom. He decided to use his new paints instead of his Daddy's spaghetti sauce!

Liz Million

Liz Million, illustrator and author of children's books, wrote and illustrated this edition of 'Digger". Liz has a wealth of book titles she has either writte or illustrated under her belt including Little Red Riding Hood, Goldilocks and the Three bears and Little Fred Riding Hood! She also travels all over the country giving talks at schools, libraries and museums.

You can see Liz's work on her web site at

www.lizmillion.com

"Hello! My name is Liz Million. I am the person that wrote and illustrated this colourful book and I hope you enjoyed my story.

I used to draw all the time as a little girl and I always knew I wanted to be an artist when I grew up- unlike poor Digger!

It takes a lot of hardwork and practise to become an illustrator. I feel like the luckiest person in the world as I get to DRAW and WRITE for a living!

When I am not working in my studio I visit lots of schools and libraries and show children how to draw and write which is brilliant!

Why not have a go at making your own story book? Perhaps try and write another book for Digger my character?

Best of luck!"

Liz Million

Caboodle Books

Caboodle Books publish a range of books from their stable of award winning authors from children's stories like 'Digger' to zany poetry and tales of magic and intrigue. Founder of Caboodle Books, Trevor Wilson, also runs Authors Abroad who organise school visits all over the world where the authors give seminars and presentations of their work.

Trevor Wilson

Between them, the authors have a host of awards and experience including TV drama and a BAFTA award for Roy Apps and his work in children's television.

If you are a budding author or poet and would like more information visit **www.authorsabroad.com**